MADELEINE'S
Mistletoe Meet Cute

ELLIE HALL

Copyright © 2024 by Ellie Hall

All rights reserved.

No part of this book may be reproduced in any form or by any electronic or mechanical means, including information storage and retrieval systems, without written permission from the author, except for the use of brief quotations in a book review.

This is a work of fiction. Names, characters, businesses, places, events, and incidents are either the products of the author's imagination or used in a fictitious manner. Any resemblance to actual persons, living or dead, or actual events is purely coincidental.

A NOTE FROM ELLIE

Dear reader,

Thank you for picking up *Madeleine's Mistletoe Meet Cute*. I hope you enjoy Maddie and Duffy's whirlwind romance.

With the hustle of the holidays, this "Short read" is the perfect length when you want a romance reading "Nibble."

In this book, you'll find a grumpy boss, a ghost baker (like a ghostwriter), and a fake relationship set in a small town. North Pole is a real place in Alaska, but I took liberties with sprinkles of "Elf dust" to make it my own.

Between the pages, you might also spot "Easter eggs," little mentions and cameos from my other books. This story will also tie into a future series I'm going to write about Maddie's sisters.

Because this is part of the Christmas Kisses and Cookie Crumbs series, the big dilemma was choosing which recipe to share. I opted for the Madeleines, but be on the lookout for the sugar cookie candy cane twists in the future.

If you enjoy this Christmas romcom or make the recipe, please spread the Christmas cheer by leaving a review and sharing on social media. Be sure to tag me. I'm @elliehallauthor everywhere.

Get something cozy to drink, snuggle up, and prepare for a heartwarming, feel-good short read filled with holly, jolly Christmas joy.

Ellie

CHAPTER 1

MADDIE

*H*ow to break your life in three easy steps:
1. Fall in love with your best friend and find out it's unrequited.
2. After leaving a store, get into the wrong car and nearly be arrested.
3. Accidentally send your boss another client's content . . . that involves kissing.

My sisters would say I'm being melodramatic. But can you blame me? This series of unfortunate events has me on the couch, surrounded by cartons of takeout and tissues. But the real travesty is I can't bring myself to decorate for Christmas.

If you know me, this is a problem of the highest magnitude. Of the four of us Tinsel girls—yes, like the shiny metallic strands that decorate Christmas that used to be popular—turns out I'm not either.

Joshy Henderson and I met in kindergarten. I always believed he was the one. Having reached thirty, my sisters said to take my shot. Either that or they were tired of me pining. They said to go for it. So I did.

I professed my undying love for Joshy. After being swept into us taking things to "The next level" and spending Thanksgiving together, he texted on Black Friday, telling me he wanted to "Drop things down to the previous level."

Ba dun, dun.

He let me down easy, but then I found out he'd been pining over his ex, Pammy, and hoped I'd help him get over her.

Pouting, I scroll social media and land on a photo taken two days ago of Joshy and Pammy back together, posing cozy at Night Lights.

It has lots of likes. Their names go nicely together, and I'm not a monster. I want him to be happy. But I thought it would be with me.

A cranky, crabby, irksome little thought that's been pestering me pokes me in the chest.

Maybe I wanted my forever fellow to be Josh because he was the *easy* button. We know each other well—seven-day summer camp without a shower friend zone status. Our inside jokes are endless. Or was that we were so comfortable with each other the problem?

The worst part of it is that we haven't been in touch since the text. I lost my best friend and the guy I thought I loved at the same time.

Pop Tart lets out a whiny bark.

"Alright, alright. I'll get my dumb butt off the couch," I say to my Chorkie. She's part Chihuahua, part Yorkshire Terrier, and all adorable beastie.

She looks at me with the sincerest puppy dog eyes on the planet.

"You're right. I shouldn't wallow."

She barks.

"Fine. I'll face the facts. Josh and I grew apart. He lives in

Connecticut. I'm here in northern New Hampshire. Our time spent together and phone call catchups had dwindled to a seasonal text, if that. And he was critical of my side hustle. All my hustles. He's probably impressed by Pam's fancy art director job.

Pop Tart's third bark is sharper this time.

Giving her lots of pets and scratchies, I say, "I never understood why he didn't like you. Who wouldn't love my little Pop Tart pupper love muffin?"

When I open the door for Pop Tart's potty break, she skitters to her spot under the holly bush. I take a breath of cool air.

Gran always said, "The best is yet to come." I tell myself to hang on. To believe it's true. There's someone out there for me to love and be loved by.

Don't get me wrong. I have a pretty great life. But with Anisette, Praline, and Tassie scattered all over the world and Gran three hours away at the Memorial Memory Care Center down in Concord, life in Liberty Lake can get a little lonely.

I love it, especially around Christmastime, but this year, everything has a bluish tint. I miss the days when Gran called us her "Sweeties." She always had cookies and milk waiting after school. We'd spend lazy summer afternoons by the lake and enjoy the "Great Christmas Celebration," as my grandfather called Gran's holiday enthusiasm.

Pop Tart hurries inside and hops onto the couch. I bring her a treat before plopping down and reviewing my internet tabs.

I stew in my recent failures, wishing I could undo them.

My main gig is the "Covert Cookie," my online business where I bake cookies for the dough-challenged or the time-limited. The kinds of people who want to be Betty Crocker, laboring all day in the kitchen baking deliciousness for their guests, friends, and family, but don't want to risk an oven fire or lawsuit.

There's also my virtual assistant side hustle. I have three

clients. Bernice Heath, the famed Regency romance author. We're on hiatus for December. Hewitt & Hershey—no relation to the chocolate, but I could go for some right now—operate an online dog accessory shop. I built their eCommerce site and help run the backend.

Pop Tart wears one of their tiny hoodies with her name embroidered on the back and looks rather adorable, if I do say so.

Last one. Worst one. Cavell Stone. Supreme Ruler of Grump Empire, Inc. Kidding. He's the CEO of a gravel, rock—or was it a coal?—company. His virtual assistant requests are sporadic, but I've handled minutia like printer ink orders to larger projects like updating old files and digitizing them without so much as a *please* or *thank you*. In real life, we'd probably despise each other. In the virtual world, I tolerate him because I need the job.

He's the one I accidentally sent Bernice's kissing scene social media image to. He was not amused. Cavell is gruff and cold. I imagine he took the empty spot at Ebenezer Scrooge's desk when *The Christmas Carol* character vacated it to have dinner with the Cratchits.

My laptop dings with a notification, but instead of a missive from Cavell, it's an inquiry from the Covert Cookie contact page.

I read the message twice.

My first thought is, *This is too good to be true.*

My second thought is, *How soon can I start?*

This could be my big break and a chance to help contribute to Gran's medical bills.

Before I get too excited about the request to supply cookies for an Annual Christmas Charity Bake & Bazaar Auction, I take a deep breath. Fingers shaking, I dial the number from the contact form.

Ten minutes later, I've agreed to supply Nicholls' Candy Cane Corp with cookies, am packing my suitcase, and have my sisters on a group call as I explain that I'll be in North Pole for Christmas this year.

I finally feel a little merry.

"You're going to bake on site?" Tassie asks.

"In Alaska!" Praline exclaims.

"What about Pop Tart?" Anisette's ex took their dog.

"To answer your rapid-fire questions, yes, the Covert Cookie is taking me to North Pole, Alaska, for a charity auction. Pop Tart was invited to come, too." My voice gets small. I know they love me, but I'm the *fa la la loser* sister who hasn't yet gotten her life together.

"I'm stuck in Little Rock, so I wouldn't be able to see you anyway," Ani says.

"I agreed to go on a ski trip to the Alps with Aldo for the holidays." Praline doesn't sound too pleased.

"Aren't you fancy?" I can't tell if Tassie is being sarcastic or not.

We're all quiet for a moment, realizing the same thing at the same time. This means Gran will be alone. The adjacent thought about Gran, I'm certain we're all having, makes my eyes damp. She no longer recognizes us and seldom acknowledges anyone, not even her caretakers.

"It's not the same as it used to be," Ani says softly.

We all agree, but we don't stay glum for more than a moment because Gran was the queen of turning our frowns upside down. She wouldn't want us to dwell on her memory loss.

By the time I get off the phone, I'm smiling at happier times in the Tinsel household when Gran was lively, and Gron—our grandad's name was Ron—was still alive.

After packing and tidying up the house, I head to the airport for a red-eye flight. Once settled in with my seatbelt fastened and my tray table in the upright position, I realize I forgot my lucky apron. For once, maybe I won't need it.

Before I power down my laptop, I receive a notification from Cavell.

> Cavell: Arrange a meeting on 12/26 with AccuPlex. I'm not pleased with the projections for next year.

I could ignore it, but I opt to spread the Christmas cheer.

> 00M: Seasons greetings! I wish you and your family a blessed Christmas. Thank you for being such a supportive and caring boss.

Gram always said *Kill 'em with kindness*. To which Gron replied, *And Bury 'em with a smile*. He was a gravedigger and had a dark sense of humor.

> Cavell: Arrange the appointment.

Well, bah humbug to you, too.

CHAPTER 2

DUFFY

I used to live by the adage, *If you want something done right, do it yourself.* But having my name, Cavell Coal, next to the letters CEO forced me to hire a virtual assistant. Nonetheless, it looks like I still have to do things myself.

It's been ten minutes. Why don't I see the meeting on my digital calendar?

The voice in my head sounds suspiciously like my mother's, *Duffy, mind your manners,* and *Life's too short not to smile and eat waffles for dinner.* I ignore it for now.

00M's silence could be because it's almost Christmas. That's a mere technicality because everyone knows the lights remain on twenty-four-seven in corporate America.

When I hired her on the recommendation of one of my mother's friends, I'll admit that I appreciated the James Bond-style gig page on the virtual assistant website. She goes by *00M*, possibly a combination of *007* and the head of the MI6 in the films. I don't play favorites, but "Golden Eye" was a masterpiece.

I ping my VA with a nudge.

> Cavell: Don't forget to make the appointment.

> OOM: Thank you for your message. This is a friendly reminder that I'm currently out of the office with no email access.

> Cavell: It says you're online. I have to talk to Dave Lipman no later than 12/26. No excuses.

> OOM: This is an autoresponder.

> Cavell: This app doesn't have that feature.

> OOM: Away until January 2. If you receive this message, please consider completing the task yourself.

So she is replying. My jaw ticks with irritation.

> Cavell: Do you want a job when you get back?

> OOM: This is a bot. The person you are trying to reach is unavailable. Yes, she'd like to keep her job.

A growl escapes from my throat. All of my previous virtual assistants lasted less than a week. She's going on six months—a record professionally and personally, not that I'm counting how long women tend to remain in my life.

My primary job is at Peak Financial in Boston, but I'm also the CEO of Stone's Coal Co. Unfortunately, I missed the energy boom of the early twentieth century. We sell novelty coal for Christmas stockings, ornaments, and provide wholesale shipments for the entertainment and theme park industries.

Stone's Coal Co. was my father's legacy, among other less savory things.

My mother used to handle the clerical work for the company before she retired.

Juggling both jobs became untenable, so I got the virtual assistant. But she's not cooperating, and I have to leave for the airport in two minutes. With an annoyed growl, I flip my laptop closed, grab my travel bag, and leave to make the biannual trek to the other side of the country.

Am I dragging my feet? Not really. I love my mother. It's her schemes and cohorts that make me keep my distance.

❄

When the plane touches down, the snowcapped mountains sparkle like sugar. The car service my VA arranged to take me north waits as expected, but she still didn't schedule the AccuPlex meeting.

I wasn't amused by the pink social media image with text about kissing with flowers and hearts all over it that she recently sent. Supposedly, it was an accident. A file snafu. Keep that romantic garbage away from me. We've never met or so much as spoken on the phone, and that's how I prefer it.

As the sleek black SUV winds along the familiar roads toward my hometown, I can't help but think about last Christmas when I brought Porsha here, believing she was the one. I was going to ask my mother for my grandmother's engagement ring and propose.

I caught her dressed as a scantily clad Mrs. Claus, making kissing noises while video-chatting with a bare-chested guy in a Santa hat. It was over.

No sooner does the enormous pine tree decked in lights and oversized bows and baubles rise from the town square come into view, than my phone rings.

Without a preamble, my mother asks, "Is that you?"

Confused, I reply, "You called me."

"I saw a sleek SUV drive by. Figured it was my fancy pants son. We have less than a week until the big day. Tell your driver to turn around and drop you off at Kringle's Market."

I'm barely inside the town limits, and she already spotted me.

"I need help with the grocery bags."

For a second, I thought she was going to ambush me with a "Meet cute"—what she calls a meet-up with a potential future Mrs. Stone. But with the company party later, her request checks out.

At this time of year, North Pole explodes from a population of about three thousand to many times that with tourists and annual visitors. I tell the driver where to find a parking spot.

My mother, Carol, fancies herself Mrs. Claus. She and her merry band of matchmaking elves are determined to find me "the one." Tried that. Failed. I trust relationships about as much as I trusted my father, which is to say not at all, not that it matters. He passed away two years ago, leaving me with a lump of coal and memories that turned out to be lies.

In Kringle's Market, I hear my mother's voice one aisle deep, speaking with a female. What is this trickery? Like James Bond, I keep a low profile and study a box of waffle mix. It's been ages since I had a waffle, a cinnamon roll, or any of my mother's baked goods.

Casually listening, the woman she's talking to says, "That's right. I just arrived." Her voice has a tinkling quality.

I shift to browse the snack display when Mom replies, but I don't hear over a shopping cart clanking by.

Her mark adds, "It's so jolly here."

It's true, and like cheesy chip dust, it kind of rubs off on you.

Mom says, "As the kids say, 'That's how we roll in North Pole.'"

Is that really what the kids say?

The woman says, "It was nice to meet you."

Mom Claus responds, "Since we're no longer strangers, I'm

having a holiday gathering tonight. Why don't you join us? Number eight, Balsam Lane. You can't miss it."

Lurking over here, I ought to remind my mother to be more cautious, though North Pole is nothing like the city. Everyone knows everyone's business, and if they don't, they will soon.

"Can I bring anything?" the woman asks.

I glimpse the edge of her dark brown hair, a red scarf, and a black coat.

My mother replies, "Just your beautiful smile. It's only a little get-together."

I can't help the sound that escapes. "Pfft." It's not. My mother's Christmas party is outrageous. After last year, I'd hoped to skip it, but the incoming forecast wasn't looking favorable, so I took an earlier flight. She'd never forgive me if I missed Christmas.

A grocery cart wheel squeaks, and a petite woman with white hair and rosy round cheeks approaches. "There's my handsome boy."

I'm over six feet and have to bend lower than I remember for a hug.

Not wanting to give my mother an opportunity to introduce me to the potential future "Mrs. Stone," I move us away from the *meat section*—not to be confused with the *meet section*, which is the rest of the store if you're my mother.

On cue, she says, "I just met the—"

"Mom—" I point to the cart.

She nods. "But she—"

"You and your matchmaking elves can save it."

"Don't tell me you're not over Lexus. She was so bony and phony," she mutters the last part.

"*Porsha* said she had a fast metabolism."

"She didn't touch any of the cookies or toffees or—"

"Mom," I say measuredly.

"Duffy," she echoes.

Oh no. Here we go.

I mount an on-the-spot preemptive strike and blurt, "Anyway, I'm seeing someone." The words drop out of my mouth like coal—what I'll be getting in my stocking for telling such a big, fat lie.

Her face brightens. "Really?"

I scrape out a nod, already hating myself for fibbing.

"Is she joining us?"

Scrubbing my hand down my face, I add, "She's hoping to get a flight."

My mother springs up and down on the balls of her feet. I downplay it, not wanting her public fuss to make the rounds on the Snowball Express, North Pole's online community gossip group.

Through the windows of Kringle Market, a woman with dark brown hair and wearing a red scarf walks by once, then backtracks as if not remembering where she parked.

For the first time in a long time, something inside me bounces.

She appears a third time, and then, arms lifted in the air, she rushes into traffic, shouting what sounds like, "Pop Tart."

CHAPTER 3

MADDIE

After a pit stop at Kringle Market for supplies and sundries for Pop Tart and me, she hops out of my rental car when she sees a horse-drawn carriage clip-clopping by.

Experience has proven she gets very excited by "Giant dogs." Unfortunately, they can't see her under *hoof,* and she risks getting trampled. As she races into the road, she looks over her shoulder as if to say, *Catch me if you can.*

I hurry, hollering, "Pop Tart, stop!"

A little girl and her brother corral my dog, preventing what could've been a *Flat Tart.* Their mom and dad exchange a look. I sense these kids have been hoping for a puppy, and, after saving the day, they may find one under the tree.

I thank them profusely and return to my car. A fit, tall man with trim brown hair and piercing blue eyes stares—equal parts Clark Kent and James Bond.

A jingle inside tingles.

On second thought, given his judgy expression, maybe he thinks I chased my dog into traffic.

Eyebrow arched, he turns on his heel.

Never mind, then.

I fuss over Pop Tart and remind her she's not allowed off-leash on public streets. Despite the near-squish experience, I marvel at this charming town. North Pole is like a winter wonderland theme park of Christmas perfection. Everywhere I look are festive details, like a mailbox for letters to Santa, a full-scale gingerbread house, full-size Nutcrackers, and the Sleigh Bell Lodge with a reindeer theme. Pop Tart and I are staying in the Prancer room.

I throw open the drapes of the window overlooking the main street that's like a real-life ceramic Christmas village, only better.

After giving Pop Tart a treat, I turn on *The Santa Claus* movie for her and check my laptop for *OOM* messages.

Not only is Cavell grumpy, he's extremely needy. A terrible combo. I'll admit that I had a little fun with my impromptu, out-of-office replies.

He needs to learn patience. Manners too. But maybe he's lonely. One of those guys who lives in a stark high rise, surrounded by metal and glass . . . and stone. It's in the name. I tell ya, it's always in the name.

Checking the time, I give Pop Tart a pet and then freshen up for my meeting with Nicole from Nicholls' Candy Canes. I expect the directions to lead me to an industrial part of town with factories, but the address is two streets over on Candy Cane Lane.

I love it here!

Lined with a giant candy cane archway tied with red ribbons, it dead ends to a storefront with a red and white striped awning festooned with red and white lights. Notably, there aren't too many people down this way.

A woman wearing a white uniform with a red and white striped silk scarf says, "You must be here for the appointment."

I nod and slide my eyes from side to side like a secret operative in *Mistletoe Mission: a James Bond Christmas*. Gron was a huge Bond fan. He even met Ian Flemming once. My sisters and I grew up watching the movies, including the originals from the 1960s. My virtual assistant username is *00M*, aka Double-Oh-M, a nod to the treasured memories of time spent with my grandfather.

The woman guides me toward a backroom where another woman in white waits. Her hair matches her outfit and her lips are bright red.

"You must be Madeleine." She extends her hand. "I'm Nicole Nicholls. Thank you for accepting my offer on such short notice."

"The Covert Cookie, at your service."

"You're confident you can do it?"

I nod. "Affirmative."

"This will be record-breaking."

"I'm up for the task."

She asks, "How do you take your cocoa?"

"Extra cream and a candy cane, please."

"I like your style." A smile appears on her thin lips.

This all feels very top-secret. Classified. We discuss details and terms.

I say, "I'll require a thirty-minute break every four hours."

She inclines her head in question.

"Personal reasons." Pop Tart has a small bladder and needs potty breaks.

Do I question the integrity of what I do as a covert cookie baker? Not as long as everyone involved is on the same page. I tend to think of it as a collaboration where a client presents their vision and I execute it. After that, I'm no longer part of the enterprise and how they present the baked goods is their business. They can give me credit or not. Usually, not.

She gazes through the glass window to the professional test kitchen. "Ever since my brother Nicholas got twisted up with

Gretel, heiress to the Gingerbread Boutique, things haven't been the same."

"I'm sorry to hear that," I say, trying to keep things professional.

"My heart is heavy. My troubles are—" She sighs.

"I'm here to help," I say assuringly.

"My yuletide is miles away." She shakes her head.

That reminds me how far I am from my family, but I can't deny that there's something special about North Pole, even though it seems I've entered a candy cane-gingerbread family feud.

Nicole gives me a tour of the kitchen with a broad stainless steel table in the middle, shelves filled with baking items, and a couple of stand mixers. After providing a list of additional supplies and ingredients that I'll need, I game plan my preparation of red and white candy cane twist cookies sprinkled with crushed candy canes.

When I get back to Sleighbell Lodge, Pop Tart snoozes as the credits roll to *Love on Thin Ice*, an adaptation of a hockey romcom series. I could snuggle up and replay it, but since I'll be spending my Christmas alone, I opt to go to the holiday party.

As if she can read my mind, my dog's eyes fly open.

"Yes, you can come. The woman I met at the market was the *more the merrier* type. I'm sure she'll adore you." I nuzzle my nose against Pop Tart's.

I freshen up and put on a festive plaid skirt and a fitted sweater. After styling my hair in a half ponytail with a bow, I slide in a pair of sparkly snowflake earrings and strike a pose in front of the mirror. "Am I party ready?"

Pop Tart barks in approval.

She wears a Hewitt & Hershey pup-shirt that says *Merry Woofmas*.

"And you look paw-some."

Off we go to Balsam Lane. Dark out now, the short drive

there is like the Night Lights back home. All that's missing is the Christmas music synced with the flashing lights. I tune the radio. "All I Want for Christmas is You" blares through the speakers, reminding me of Joshy and Pammy. But I'm on the other side of the world, on the eve of what I'm dubbing Bake-mas, and they can pound coal for all I care.

I park behind a long line of cars. Chin up, this change of plans is just what I need to get into the holiday spirit. I've arrived at Christmas Central with each house trying to outdo the last until I reach number eight—the crown jewel, bedecked in lights and glowing penguins, polar bears, snowmen, and Santa's elves. Spinning in a small circle, my sisters and I would've loved this place when we were kids.

From inside, the rise and fall of laughter filters through "Rocking Around the Christmas Tree." This is better than being home with the Christmas blues or holing up in the hotel all night.

The only problem is, I don't know anyone. But the mingling guests fade from my awareness in one of those slow-motion movie moments when I spot the man from outside the market. He sips from a mug of mulled cider as the lights twinkle. My heart tugs me forward as a path clears between us. He tilts his head slightly, and our eyes lock.

There's a jingle inside of me.

Could this be it?

Is this love at first sight?

My thoughts scramble the closer I get.

Then, a woman wearing a slinky red dress slides between us and stops square in front of him. She has a severe bob haircut, and her shoulder blades protrude from her back, reminding me of a gargoyle.

The bubble bursts. Pop Tart lets out a low growl.

I whisper, "Yeah, me too."

However, the man steps aside and says, "You made it."

I can't help but look around. When no other obvious "You" appears, I point at myself. Tongue-tied, I mouth, *Me?*

"I was looking for my favorite Pop Tart," he coos, reaching for my dog. Then he adds, "And my favorite Christmas present."

He's even more handsome up close, but before I can fully appreciate this, the room turns fuzzy as he leans toward me. If I didn't know better, I'd think he was about to kiss me on the forehead. Wild and hopeful ideas spring in my mind.

He whispers, "Please play along."

Pop Tart licks my arm as if insisting I say, *Yes*.

CHAPTER 4

DUFFY

I'm the kind of guy who's cool under pressure. I remain composed, confident, and clear-headed. Except right now. The wires cross. My thoughts turn into a blend of ambrosia and Aunt Mildred's fruit cake.

The moment I saw Pop Tart's owner again, something brightened inside of me. Then I heard a cackle of the Halloween variety and not the *ho ho ho holiday* kind.

While my mother, aka Mrs. Claus, and her merry band have been raving about the sweet young woman Mom met at the market, I'm doing my best not to scowl. I can't help it now. Why is Porsha, who single-handedly ruined me for romance, at the company holiday party?

However, in the presence of Pop Tart's owner, a peculiar sensation draws my lips upward. I'm afraid I look like Buddy the Elf at best and the Grinch at worst. I've never cared about my appearance, but I put in solid gym time and take weekend hikes.

"Cavell, it's such a treat to see you," Porsha purrs.

"Duffy, I see you've met Madeleine." My mother bobbles over with a tray of mini pastries.

Like a ping-pong ball that's had too much of Uncle Keith's

eggnog, I'm not sure where to look except away from Porsha and toward the woman with sparkling eyes and brown hair.

The little dog barks as if to remind me to breathe. My hairbrained plan from earlier snaps back into place. I take a long sip of mulled cider, regrouping.

"Madeleine." My tone sounds like a question rather than a statement.

Her eyes widen slightly.

I chortle. "Of course, I know Madeleine."

"You do?" I can't tell who speaks, but there's an echo.

I gingerly sling my arm across her shoulders. "And Pop Tart. Earlier in town, she tried to escape—" I hint, recalling our Main Street encounter earlier.

"Cavell saved the day." The way Madeleine's tone drops when she says my name makes me feel like I just got sprayed with cold, slushy water.

My mother studies me for a long moment. "We met at the market."

I add, "And we met about a month ago."

"Right after Thanksgiving," Madeleine clarifies.

I click my tongue. "It was one of those things."

"When you know, you know." She beams a beautiful smile that sells it for anyone watching. Wow! She's good.

Brimming with hope, Mom says, "Then it was meant to be."

"Well, it's casual," I say.

"Casual?" Madeleine asks, her voice pinched.

"But you brought her here to meet your mother." Porsha pouts.

Ah, she did understand what last year's trip meant.

"And what brings you to our home today, Lexus?" my mother asks my ex.

Porsha simpers a smile. "I was hoping to catch up with Cavell-poo."

I grimace-gag because she never called me that.

Cavell-poo? Madeleine mouths. "Funny, you never mentioned you dated someone named after a car. Must have high miles."

I nearly choke on my mulled cider.

Porsha huffs. I don't know why she's here and don't care, but I'm tangled up in tinsel now.

My ex's smile slips. "By the way, Cavell, I'm here because I work for New Face PR. Since Stone's Cole Co. needs an image upgrade, I figured I'd stoke the fires."

"How unfortunate," I mutter.

She winks. "It looks like we'll be working closely together."

"Actually, my assistant will help with that."

"Well, you know me. I'm very hands-on." She flutters her false lashes.

Madeleine's eyes bulge. "I'm certain Cavell-poo's virtual assistant can handle it. No need for you to get your hands anywhere in this vicinity." She splays her fingers and swipes the air in front of me. Her cheeks turn the faintest pink as if she likes what she sees.

Not going to lie. I do with her fair skin, long hair, and the way her skirt hugs her curves.

Porsha looks Madeleine up and down, her expression dripping with judgment. Sure, she doesn't fit the profile of previous women I'd dated in the city, but we're in North Pole where cute trumps fancy.

"Oh, look. You two are under the mistletoe." Mom points. She takes Pop Tart from my arms, probably as collateral to make sure Madeleine sticks around.

Porsha cocks her hip as if daring me to make a choice. It's a no-brainer.

I turn to Madeleine. "Looks that way."

Her sparkling eyes tip upward. "So we are."

Our gazes meet for one long moment that stops time. My pulse slows. Her breath catches.

I slide a piece of her hair from her cheek. "Can I kiss you?"

She lifts onto her toes and whispers into my ear. "What's going on?"

Her warm breath tickles my neck. "Can I explain later?"

Once more, our eyes float together, and she gives a subtle nod.

Before our lips meet, Porsha storms off.

But that doesn't stop our collision course. The space between us disappears, and my lips meet hers. They're soft, willing, and make me rethink what I thought I knew about kissing and connection and Christmas.

One touch, and this is all I've ever wanted. Ever needed. I feel like a cliché, but my thoughts quickly fade, dropping me fully into this moment under the mistletoe.

My fingers lightly trace her jaw, and her palms press softly against my chest. Our bodies are tentative, but our mouths know what we want and it's very much mutual.

When we shift, our noses brush. Her cheeks lift with a smile that draws something out of me I haven't felt in a long time. My pulse quickens. My chest rattles and knocks like it's humming to life after a cold winter's slumber.

This is longer than a customary kiss under the mistletoe, but we lean into it as if neither one of us ever wants it to end.

CHAPTER 5

MADDIE

Cavell, my boss, also known as Duffy, cups my cheek so tenderly that I almost don't believe he's the same person. Must be a lookalike. Or a dream. Is this the Land of Sweets? Did I travel here on the Polar Express?

No matter how much that little voice of insecurity tries to talk me out of this—okay, there might be some logic piping up, too—my body knows what it wants.

My mouth melts into his and everything turns to liquid—my thoughts, my pulse, my entire body puddles into his embrace as his palms find the small of my back and tug me closer.

The kiss deepens for three, two, one, and then my awareness slips back.

Ordinarily, I'd never do something so bold and brazen, but mistletoe rules are rules and maybe this is a minor Christmas miracle.

Cavell is incredibly handsome.

And a grump.

But an amazing kisser.

And my boss.

My thoughts slide back and forth like a snowball in a pinball machine.

The sparks were flying and now they're fizzling as I draw away and back to sanity.

Our eyes meet and linger for a long beat before I search his for recognition. Does he know that I'm *00M*? Guilt takes the shape of a black lump of coal in my belly. I have to tell him the truth.

The whole room is quiet for the length of a breath, then they erupt into cheers, with Carol being the loudest of all. She got her Christmas wish, that's for sure.

Don't get me wrong, I understand why the guy is single, at least from working as his assistant, but I don't *see* why he's single.

Cavell is fit, his posture is pure confidence, and his lips are what dreams are made of. Only, I'm awake and we kissed.

I kissed my boss.

Panic replaces the warm, cozy feeling from under the mistletoe.

A flush creeps along his neck. I'm certain my cheeks match at least a third of the Christmas décor in this room with the red, white, and green theme—I'm a mishmash of warm all over, white as a sheet, and green around the gills.

When everyone goes back to their merry-making, Cavell—or is it Duffy?—says, "I have to admit, we make a good team."

Being his employee and all, I bite my tongue, afraid now is not the moment to reveal my identity with Carol glowing at the good news that her son has a girlfriend. A fake one who also happens to work for him, but they don't know that . . . yet.

I exhale a nervous laugh. "I couldn't agree more."

"Thank you for going along with it."

I poke him in the stomach. My finger springs back from his rock-solid abs and stings a little. "Ouch." I rub it, then say, "So you do have manners."

The space between his eyebrows pinches. "You met my mother at the market?"

"Earlier today."

"Are you from town?"

"No, I'm visiting on assignment through Christmas. I take it you're from here." Which defies everything I assumed about this man. I imagined him living in a sterile, impersonal chamber made for vampires.

"Born and raised, if you can believe that."

"I cannot," I mutter. Then louder, I say, "So is it Cavell or Duffy?"

He winces and then tilts his head for me to follow him out of the living room. The house is best described as grand, and I imagine there's a body of water nearby with a dock and a beautiful view.

Oh, Cavell—or Duffy—who are you?

We pass through the kitchen, where festive platters, plates, and bowls cover every surface and are filled with everything from fruit compote with brie to fudge. My mouth waters, but my healthy appetite takes the backseat because I need answers. I should also 'fess up, but why ruin a good thing even if it's fake?

Are my ethics and morals in the dumpster by not telling my boss who I really am? Maybe for one night, I can pretend I have my life together.

Is that so bad? Probably. Definitely.

I promise myself I'll fix it. However, the little matter of omission with the tall, broad-shouldered man makes me fear I'll soon get a visit from the ghosts of Christmas past, present, and future if I'm not careful.

We exit the warm kitchen into the chilly night on the back deck. My breath instantly clouds as Cavell-Duffy inhales deeply. Jaw set, he doesn't speak right away. Given what I know about him, he's a man of few words.

"So, it's casual, huh?" I say, breaking the silence.

"Huh?" he repeats, perhaps not recalling his earlier comment.

"Our fake relationship," I add.

He brushes his hand across his forehead. "When I saw Porsha—"

"Porsha? I thought her name was Lexus."

"My mother intentionally doesn't remember her name. She'd like to forget about my ex altogether. I would. Then you came over, and something came over me." He shifts uncomfortably, "I'm not usually like this. It's this place. . ."

"Christmas Town?"

"Being back in North Pole, I can't explain it. But I can explain the kiss."

"Is that so? If fireworks were a classic Christmas tradition, they would've blown off the roof, which would be a shame because this is a lovely home." I admire our surroundings.

His eyes widen as if he's not easily surprised and a faint smile feathers his lips. "You're not wrong."

"So *casual*. . ." I repeat, struggling with how to broach the subject of being *OOM*.

Letting out a foggy breath, he says, "Serious. Casual. I don't know. Porsha was the first woman I brought home. I thought she was the one and then learned she was cheating on me."

Not seeing any residual pain in his expression, I say, "You probably dodged a snowball with that one."

He snorts a laugh. "You got that right."

His blue eyes sweep mine, snagging me in the best of ways and making me want to linger.

"While we're on the topic of exes, I recently got let down hard as opposed to being let down easy." I tell him about the best friend-to-not-love situation.

"Sorry about that, but I'm glad you were available for the kiss."

"Happy to help. Now what?" I ask vaguely, knowing the end

of the sentence dangles with what I should be telling him about being his assistant.

He puffs his cheeks.

Silence threads between us as the happy sounds of the party filter from inside.

I bounce a little, chilly. "So, are you Cavell or Duffy?"

This would be a moment for him to answer, offer me a jacket, or both. Instead, he plants his hand on my lower back.

A ray of warmth beams through me.

He says, "We should go inside."

"'Tis the season to be freezin,'" I say, teeth chattering.

The corner of his lip lifts.

Back in the cozy kitchen, he pours me a mug of warm mulled cider and fixes me a plate. "I know you're perfectly capable of picking out the foods you'd like, but I've been attending these shindigs all my life. You want to avoid the calamari salad and if you're not quick, you'll miss the pecan bacon pinwheels which only appear once a year."

Touched by his thoughtfulness, I happily take the plate. Where I expect him to excuse himself and mingle with the guests, he guides me through a door off the kitchen and into a library with floor-to-ceiling shelves and a stained glass lamp between two comfy-looking chairs.

He closes the door, muffling the faint strains of "Deck the Halls" playing and the laughter overflowing from the party. A fire crackles in the hearth.

"Sorry about the chill. I needed a breath of fresh air."

"It's toasty in here."

"Always my favorite room." Then, as if getting down to business, he says, "My name is Cavell Duibhshíth Stone—my father was Irish."

"He was Cavell Senior?"

Bristling slightly, he nods. "Correct. Professionally, I go by

Cavell. Everyone here calls me Duffy—a shortened version of my middle name."

With the warm firelight scene, I don't want to ruin the moment, so like a *liar, liar, pants on fire* for omitting our connection, I ask, "Can I call you Duffy?"

He smirks. "Sure."

Extending my hand to shake, he clasps it, defrosting my cold fingers and sending a thrill of warmth across my skin.

"It's nice to meet you, Duffy. I'm Madeleine Tinsel, but my family and friends call me Maddie, Maddiesaurus, or Maddie Cakes."

His chuckle lengthens a little like he's knocking the ice off it.

"What brings you here for the holidays, Maddie?"

Not sure how much I should reveal, I answer, "I was hired to do some baking. It's not the usual arrangement, but I couldn't say no."

"So you're a baker?"

"Among other things. I have a few jobs. Technically, I'm a ghost baker. Clients hire me to bake cookies when they aren't able for a host of reasons, but they get the credit."

"Like a ghostwriter?"

I tap the air. "You get the concept."

"It's genius."

I tuck my chin with surprise. "Thank you. My ex-best friend said the idea was 'half baked.'"

He frowns, "Since you won't be with your family for Christmas Eve or Christmas Day, you're welcome to join us."

Cavell Duffy Stone—I'm not going to attempt his middle name—is not who I expected. I have to come clean. But I can't, instead of confessing. I say, "Thank you. That would be lovely."

I should be thinking about how wrong our mistletoe moment was, but I can't help wonder about the mistletoe potential.

CHAPTER 6

DUFFY

The highs and lows from the company party filter back. My thoughts cling to the mistletoe kiss with Madeleine like the snow on the windowpanes of my childhood bedroom.

With three days before Christmas Eve, I'm lucky I beat the storm because it'll be a whiteout at this rate. I could've done without Porsha's unwelcome appearance. But meeting Maddie is a different story, one I don't quite understand. There's something familiar about her. It's like we're instantly comfortable with each other. Maybe that's what happens when you start things with a kiss. I remind myself it's fake.

But her lips on mine felt very, very real.

I check the virtual assistant portal to see if *OOM* added the meeting with AccuPlex to my schedule, but she's offline.

When I get downstairs, the remnants of the party are cleaned up thanks to my muscles and my mother's merry elves. However, she's already in the kitchen, making my favorite: waffles with blueberries and fresh whipped cream. Every summer, I used to pick them on our property.

"You're smiley this morning."

Usually, I'm nothing short of stony, at least until I have coffee. Goes with the name, I guess. Or so I thought. "Don't know what you're talking about."

"You look cheerful, wistful . . . and in love."

The coffee sloshes as I pour a cup. "I wouldn't go that far."

"Madeleine was lovely. The perfect future daughter-in-law."

I pump my hands. "Let's not get ahead of ourselves."

"After you went to bed last night, I polished your grandmother's ring. It's ready and available."

"Mom! We only met—"

She gives me a look.

"I mean, it's new." Very new.

"You have a certain spark and that kiss—" She fans her face.

"Mom!" I echo.

She slides a waffle onto my plate and pecks the top of my head. She spoils me and her affection is always appreciated. After seeing Porsha again, I can't fathom a future with her. Maddie was right. I dodged that snowball.

My ex didn't want a family. I do, but I'm afraid because I don't want to turn out like my father. I picture him now, seated across the table, a waffle at his place setting and the newspaper in front of his nose. My mother deserved better than a cheater.

Last Christmas, instead of cheer, I found out he had another wife and a daughter in Ireland.

A thought breaks through the walls I've built around myself after learning of his mistress and brightens like the lights on the tree. Since I now know how devastating being cheated on was, it's like an inoculation against turning out like him.

"An extra dollop of fresh whipped cream for your thoughts?" Mom asks.

"Thinking about Dad."

"Not a day passes when I don't." She sighs and lowers into a chair.

"Mom, I want—"

Interrupting me, she meets my gaze. "I never wanted to have to discuss this. I knew."

Of course, she did. My heart craters for her.

"We did our best to work through it. I couldn't fully trust him again, but I did forgive him. Best of all, I got you out of it."

The ache goes deeper.

"Duffy, it's not your burden to bear. You're not Cavell. You're my son, and whether you settle down with Madeleine or —please not Lexus—"

"You have my word," I say.

We share a laugh.

"You'll make a wonderful and loyal husband . . . and a father too—"

In the past, I would've objected, however, a woman with silky brown hair, a warm gaze, and curves for days floats into my mind and lingers there like she plans to stick around.

"In the meantime, I don't think we need Lexus to be the new face of anything. I have an idea," Mom says, referring to the PR firm I asked my assistant to hire.

"I have Stone's Coal Company under control. My VA has been digitizing everything. Soon, our office will be virtual, which will make it easier for me to manage things remotely."

"I'm like a windup music box rather than one of your streaming devices. Old school. We need to keep Stone's Coal in the community, so I signed you up for the Annual Christmas Charity Bake & Bazaar Auction."

I nearly choke on a bite of my waffle. "You what?"

"You'll contribute a baked good and go to the gala on Christmas Eve."

I press my lips together to summon patience. "Mom, have you met me?"

Wearing a quizzical expression, she loads my plate with another waffle. "Of course."

"Then you're aware the kitchen, no less baking, is not in my wheelhouse."

"The Stones can do anything they put their mind to. Figure it out."

And that's how my mother always ends a conversation that's not up for debate. My thoughts drift to Madeleine. Then I get an idea. Maybe she can help.

No sooner am I in the old pickup truck I've had since high school do I realize that I don't know where to find Maddie. She mentioned baking and accepted my invitation to spend the holidays together. This brings up two additional issues: continuing to fake our relationship and being my guest at the gala.

I thought I was tangled up in tinsel before. Now I'm buried in it.

If I were an adorable, beautiful woman from out of town, where would I be?

Never mind. I spot Maddie in the town center by the massive Christmas tree with her little dog. She's talking to Mrs. Hershey. Eyes bright, Maddie laughs. The sound of it filters toward me from last night. It's a lovely tinkle. Not a cackle at all. She's everything that Porsha isn't.

I park and hurry down the sidewalk before skidding to a stop as Maddie waves goodbye to Mrs. Hershey.

She beams a smile. "I guess this is the corner to run into people. That was Cheryl Hershey, Sherry Hershey's sister of Hewitt & Hershey fame—not the chocolate company."

I scratch my head, not quite following.

"Pop Tart is wearing one of their custom collars." She scoops the dog into her arms. "I work—" She cuts herself off. "I should probably get to work. Lots of baking to do."

"About that, do you mind if we walk and talk? I have a question."

"You're a businessman even on Christmas vacation." She seems vaguely disappointed.

"True, and that's what this is about. I know my strengths. They do not include baking, but my mother signed me up—well, Stone's Coal Company—for the Annual Christmas Charity Bake & Bazaar Auction." I go on to explain the event.

She taps the air with her finger and then leans in. "I probably shouldn't tell you this, but I was hired to ghost bake for a local business for that very auction. If we're going to have this conversation, I need chocolate. A hot chocolate," she clarifies.

After Maddie drops Pop Tart off at the Sleigh Bell Lodge, we cross the street to Frosty's Festive Flavors Bakery & Café. I hold open the door, imagining she welcomes the warmth after the North Pole chill.

Maddie orders a salted caramel mocha latte with chocolate shavings. I stick with my usual black coffee.

"I love how much the people in North Pole embrace Christmas." She glances at my drink. "Almost everyone."

"They wouldn't have it any other way."

"You don't count yourself as a North Pole-ian? North Pole-ite? One of Santa's elves?" she laughs.

Even though I've heard all the North Pole jokes, I do too. Something about Maddie brings a smile to my face, chases away the shadows and doubts, and whatever keeps me in the dark—she's like a human candle, bright and glowing.

We find a vacant table, and I pull out the chair for her.

As if surprised by my gentlemanliness, she says, "Thank you, Duffy."

I take a seat and lower my voice, "My baking business proposal for you—"

"For the Covert Cookie," she corrects.

"The what?"

"That's the name of my company. You can visit my website if you want to make an official inquiry."

I tilt my head in question.

She nods, gesturing I pull out my phone. "In the spirit of keeping things professional, Mr. Businessman."

When I find TheCovertCookie.com, I enter my information.

Moments later, her phone dings with a notification. She checks it and her eyebrows lift. "You want me to make cookies on behalf of Stone's Coal Company for the charity auction. What's your vision? You didn't fill out the questionnaire."

She's my vision. Giving my head a little shake, I say, "Cookies."

"Can you be more specific?"

I wince. "I figured you could make some chocolate chip or oatmeal. The little bits look like coal, right?"

"The object of the auction is to raise money. You want your donation to go to the highest bidder. Although chocolate chip, oatmeal raisin, or even a combo are undeniably delicious, I don't think they'll get the big bucks."

"What do you propose?"

"I'll have to think about it."

"We only have a couple of days until the event."

"And I have to head over to work."

"How about after you're done? We can brainstorm or experiment."

"It's a deal." She extends her hand to shake, then quickly retracts it. In a whisper, she asks, "If so, are we still a couple? It would be weird for people to see us shaking hands."

Considering my mother spotted me the second I arrived in town, I don't want the fake dating arrangement to get back to her via the Snowball Express. I nod and pat Maddie's hand instead.

She laughs. "You're terrible at selling this. Do you want to be a fake couple or not?"

I want to, but doubt peppers my mind.

Maddie's eyes flash over my shoulder and she hisses, "Avalanche, incoming."

Before I can ask questions or answer, Porsha saunters over.

Inside, I deflate.

"Look, it's North Pole's local love birds."

"What a pleasure seeing you again, Mercedes, was it?" Madeleine asks.

I almost spit out my coffee from laughter.

"Porsha," she corrects. "I was preparing myself for the charity auction. I applied to be a judge. I made a great impression on Richard Loomis last year." She bats her eyelashes.

That old codger? "What an unpleasant surprise." My tone drops with displeasure.

"Cavell-poo, I thought what we had was special, long-lasting, forever."

Given Porsha's appraising gaze, I sense she doesn't believe that Maddie and I are together.

Madeleine lengthens her spine. "My sister recently found a cockroach in her shower cap."

I frown because that's downright disturbing.

Porsha's brow furrows.

"She freaked out but then put on her big girl britches—not literally because she was in the shower. She washed that roach down the drain. Some things in life are like that. You have to say buh-bye." Madeleine opens and closes her hand, waving goodbye.

Porsha staggers, likely never having been dismissed before.

While I'm not sure where Maddie and I stand, things are officially over with my ex. It's been a year. As my mother said, I can forgive her, but I cannot forget nor can I trust her.

I say, "To put it another way, if you'd please excuse my girlfriend and me, we're enjoying some time together, alone."

Porsha lets out a whiny huff and stomps her foot, likely having realized what Madeleine meant about the roach as she stomps off.

We both stifle laughter. "I'm sorry if that was mean-spirited, but she was insulting me—and our fake relationship."

"I apologize for not coming to your defense sooner. *Our* defense."

"So, I'm your girlfriend?" she singsongs.

"I feel a little old to be someone's boyfriend."

"How old are you?"

"I'm thirty-four."

"I'm newly thirty."

"What else should I know about you Madeleine Tinsel, owner of the Covert Cookie?"

"About that, um, I have something to tell you. Or maybe I should show you." She shuffles nervously.

I caught Porsha red-handed, er, in a skimpy Mrs. Claus suit doing a video call with her other boyfriend. I don't think Madeleine is cheating on our fake relationship, but my stomach sinks because I fear whatever Maddie will reveal won't make my spirits bright.

CHAPTER 7

MADDIE

The main downtown area of North Pole is relatively compact, but with Duffy in the passenger seat, I find my way to Stone's Coal Company on the outskirts.

"What are we doing here?" he asks.

Taking a deep breath, I answer, "Remember how Porsha said your virtual assistant hired her PR firm to improve media relations and increase content marketing?"

"Wait. How'd you know those details?"

I wince. Here goes. "Because I'm *00M*. I hired Porsha, which means I'm firing her, but—"

He goes stone still. "If you're my virtual assistant. That means I'm your boss."

"Technically, it's contractual work, but—"

Duffy's expression cycles through surprise, disbelief, and lands somewhere undefined. "But you're on vacation."

"You are, too."

He wipes his brow. "This is—"

"A small world?"

"When did you realize—?"

"At the Christmas party."

"Why'd you go along with it?"

"Because I need the job and you needed help."

"This is outrageous."

"I understand if you want to fire me."

He scrubs his hand through his hair. "Technically, your contract renews on January first. You're a free agent."

"True. I forgot about that since you'd sent me a task the other day. I hope there are no hard feelings."

He grunts. "There are feelings, alright."

I nod slowly, entirely unsure where this is going. "Am I getting Cavell, stone-cold businessman, or Duffy, the fun Christmas fan?"

He gazes fixedly out the window.

When he doesn't answer, I offer a sincere apology. "I'm sorry."

He nods sharply. "I still need the cookies. Are you okay with that?"

My stomach drops like I unwrapped a gift to find the box empty. Joshy thought that would be funny one year. "Yes. Of course. For your part, I want you to attempt to make your coal cookie which will give us a starting point."

He shakes his head, then shifts to nodding. "But where does this leave us?"

"Do you mean as a fake couple?"

He nods.

"Game on."

That afternoon, I go on autopilot while baking and twisting the candy cane dough in Nicholls' kitchen. I don't think about Duffy when a man in flannel enters the shop, looking for a gift or when a couple nuzzles noses while waiting to check out. Nope. This is a Duffy and me free zone.

He said he had feelings. Knowing him, they're probably icy. Although, he did accept my apology.

The baking timer buzzes, and I startle, realizing it's been

going off like an alarm. I could use my lucky apron right now . . . or my sisters. But there's no time to stop if I'm going to stay on schedule and have time to help Duffy later.

When later comes, nerves jangle around inside, following me from the Sleigh Bell Lodge, where I freshen up and get Pop Tart through town to Balsam Lane.

I park in the driveway and take a few deep breaths. "What's the worst that could happen?"

Pop Tart tilts her head and barks.

"You're right. I already had a mistletoe meet-cute with the guy who turned out to be my boss, and for the last twenty-four hours, I've been faking a relationship with him. Could this go further south? Considering we're in North Pole, technically, yes, so please don't answer that question."

My Chorkie remains quiet.

Drawing a deep breath, I say, "Let's do this."

I expect Carol to greet me at the door, but it's Duffy, wearing a slate gray V-neck sweater with a white dress shirt underneath and deep cranberry pants. He seems subdued, which is exactly what I'd expect from Cavell. When I set down Pop Tart, she rushes toward him. He crouches and proceeds to do what can best be described as "playing dog."

It's adorable.

Two points for Pop Tart. At least he likes her. I tell myself I only care because I'm his virtual assistant and can't afford to lose my job.

"Is something cooking, er, burning?"

He rubs the back of his neck. "My mother is at an ornament exchange, leaving me alone in the kitchen as you requested."

"Don't tell me you—?"

He frowns. "I don't know what I did, but it's not good."

"Let's see the damage."

I follow Duffy toward the kitchen and he stops abruptly in the entryway. I bump into him and stagger backward at the same time he reaches for my arm. Jolly little jingle tingles rush through me, but they're at odds with his grave expression.

"Sorry about that," he says.

"No, I bumped into you and—"

At the same time, we both notice what hangs from the ceiling.

His eyes shadow with concern. "Not sure how that got there."

"The mystery of the moving mistletoe," I joke.

Duffy almost smiles. Then he straightens and says, "About the cookies. I tried. Honest."

"You mean you didn't purposefully bake a bad batch so I'd make them for you?"

"Definitely not. But . . ."

"Can I see?"

"First, I want to apologize for how I was acting earlier. Coming back here is like a throat punch."

"That's extreme. Nothing about North Pole comes across as particularly dangerous."

"You do want to watch out for moose, especially during mating season."

He cracked a joke.

"I always thought this place, my family, was untouchable. Last Christmas, I found out my father cheated repeatedly."

"On Carol?! She could be Mrs. Claus's twin."

"Exactly. Throat punch. Being here brings that to the surface. But this year, it's different, which confuses me."

"Are you trying to say we made a terrible first impression in the virtual world, we were both mistaken and want to try again in real life?"

A broad grin spreads across Duffy's mouth. "Yes, that."

I slip under his arm and into the kitchen. He rushes after me, tickling my sides, but before I writhe with laughter, I stop short. I half expect a disaster, like a snow squall with legs passed through the room, but everything is tidy except for the contents of the serving platter on the counter.

I gasp. "What. Are. Those?"

"Coal cookies," Duffy murmurs.

Pop Tart, ever the fan of being underfoot for scraps, marches in and then right back out.

I examine the brown, lumpen shapes. "They look like—"

He rushes toward me, shaking his head. "Don't say it."

"But I can't unsee it."

"Can we pretend this never happened?"

I cast my gaze upward, meeting his eyes. "Which part?"

He bites the corner of his lip and marches me backward. "Everything before we met under the mistletoe."

"I did get a terrible first impression of you. A cold, calculating, miserly businessman," I say playfully, tugging on his shirt.

He taps my nose. "You were a flighty, not very efficient virtual assistant who sent me a social media post about a kissing scene."

I bite my lip.

His eyelids get heavy and his focus drops to my mouth.

Once more, we're under the mistletoe.

My heart races as I suck in a breath.

He leans forward and then the door flies open.

CHAPTER 8

DUFFY

*M*y mother bursts through the door and exclaims, "You found the mistletoe!"

A flush creeps up my neck toward my ears. Nothing like being back home, huh?

Pop Tart lets out a happy yelp.

Flustered, Maddie smooths her hair.

"As you were," Mom says.

I offer a pathetic little shrug and stammer, "Sorry about that."

"I should, um—" Maddie turns in a slow circle.

When facing me again, we both burst into stifled, snorty laughter like two teenagers who were caught and are now on Santa's naughty list.

For once, I haven't done anything wrong. Our kiss at the party felt right, even if under fake pretenses. All the same, I'm not sure what to think. Embarrassed at being caught? But I like Maddie a lot. So much that I can't be upset about her keeping quiet about being my VA.

I walk Maddie and Pop Tart to the car. We say a lingering goodnight. I'm counting down the hours until I see her again.

❄

*I*t's the day before Christmas Eve, and Madeleine is at the Nicholls' kitchen baking, leaving me to do some chores for my mother around the house—and hiding the step ladder. There will be no more climbing or moving the mistletoe.

While in the garage, I find my old toboggan. I clean it off as I formulate a plan. Last night, Maddie and I agreed to forget about my attempt to make coal cookies and regroup later today. After scouring the internet for ideas, I came up with one. While I'd like to do it myself and surprise her, I've proven that I'm a kitchen menace, so I'll need her help.

First, I bring her a red, white, and green panini during her lunch break—a woman cannot live on cookies alone, though I imagine she'd argue that, especially this time of year.

Because this is a Covert Cookie operation, I try to be stealthy, channeling James Bond, but she spots me through the crack in the door, whisks it open, and tugs me inside.

"No one can see you since you're technically the competition."

"The charity auction isn't cutthroat." I jiggle the paper bag. "I brought you lunch."

She peers inside. "It smells divine."

The corner of my mouth twitches toward a smile. "If only I could take credit. The wizards at *Buon Natale* Deli made it."

"Do you mean elves? After all, this is North Pole."

This year, my heart is a little softer, less grinchy.

While she eats the sandwich, I survey the trays of cookies. "You're making good progress."

"Nicole added a couple dozen. She wants this to be a big, splashy comeback for the candy cane store."

I sit on a counter stool. "Why do you keep your cookie business a secret?"

"It goes with the territory. The whole brand is built around discretion."

"Don't you want to be a famous baking star like on HLTV?"

Maddie wipes her fingers on a napkin. "No, I want to do my part to help pay my grandmother's medical bills. My sisters all contribute. One is a single mom. Another has huge student loans and the third was recently laid off. Tough times for everyone."

An idea floats into my mind like a snowflake and melts into the one I had earlier during my cookie research.

Maddie fiddles with a measuring spoon. "I only feel capable when I'm making cookies. Those I get right. Like how peanut butter and chocolate go together. Baking and I are the perfect match. If you disagree, we can still be friends." She smiles thinly, but the humor doesn't meet her eyes. "I should get back to work."

I tip her chin up with the crook of my finger. "*OOM*, you're good at more than baking. Can you spare a half hour? Five minutes is hardly a break." I want to show Maddie how much I appreciate her.

She bites her lip. "Is this Cavell speaking or—?"

"It's a guy who likes cookies, especially peanut butter and chocolate chip. Our errand is for the gala, which is part of the charity event. First, there's dinner, then the auction, followed by dessert and dancing. I was hoping you'd be my date."

Her lips quirk with a grin. "Is this Duffy talking?"

"Definitely."

"If I combine the errand with dropping by the Sleigh Bell Lodge to check on Pop Tart, I can spare thirty minutes, not a second longer, otherwise, I'll fall behind."

"After our stop, I can bring Pop Tart back to my house. My mother would love some company." As we walk through town, I tell Maddie about Mittens, our old Saint Bernard. "After Dad passed away, she started making Mittens homemade meals. That dog was spoiled."

"Your mom is the sweetest. She reminds me a bit of Gran, but younger." Maddie tells me about how her grandmother is in a memory care center. "My sisters and I were all foster children that she adopted."

"She sounds like an amazing woman."

"She and Carol would be best friends, given their shared love for all things Christmas."

We stroll down the sidewalk and approach a rustic sporting goods store that was one of the first three shops in town from the frontier days.

"Outdoor Outfitters probably won't have what we're looking for. But Mary's Ribbons & Threads will do the trick."

The space between Maddie's brow wrinkles as we enter.

Mary, one of my mother's matchmaking elves, practically croons, "It's North Pole's latest couple. That kiss under the mistletoe was so romantic."

My ears heat. "Hi, Mrs. Woodward. I take it you remember Madeleine."

"How could I forget." She lowers her voice to a whisper, "She outshines Lexus by a mile."

I don't want to think about my ex. "Maddie needs something to wear to the gala, but she's short on time. It'll have to be quick."

Mrs. Woodward squeals with delight. "That's Christmas music to my ears, but you can't rush these things. Duffy, be on your way. I'll take good care of our Maddie." Turning to my fake girlfriend, she says, "Welcome to the family. We're glad to have you."

Madeleine peers over her shoulder, eyes wide.

I wave because she's in good hands. "See you at six for dinner."

Stopping at Kringle's Market, I pick up a few items, place a pizza delivery order for six-thirty, and then grab Pop Tart before heading home.

MADELEINE'S MISTLETOE MEET CUTE

When the doorbell rings a few hours later, I startle, having given my full focus to the jigsaw puzzle Mom and I are doing. Pop Tart beats me to the door, turning in happy circles.

My mother calls, "I adore the pitter-patter of little feet."

"Doesn't that saying apply to children?"

"A grandmother-to-be can only hope."

Like the puzzle on the table, a future with Maddie takes shape, one I wouldn't mind piecing together with her.

Mom and I get an earful from Maddie about Mrs. Woodward's insistence that the colors burgundy and cream are her best friends. Then she turns to me. "You didn't have to get me a dress."

My mother asks, "Did you pack anything for a gala?"

"No, but I can't have my bo—" Madeleine goes quiet and swallows the rest of the word *boss*. "My boyfriend, um—" Her eyes dart my way.

"I'm glad to hear my son is a gentleman. It can be hard to accept the generosity of others, but it's Christmas, the season for gift-giving. I have dinner with the ladies, so I'd better get ready."

This is the first I've heard about my mother's plans tonight, but she scurries off.

"Sorry, I almost blew it," Maddie whispers.

"I'll tell her the truth." But it'll break her heart.

"Maybe after I leave?"

Ignoring the ever-looming future, I usher us into the kitchen.

Maddie rubs her hands together. "Ooh la la. You know how to woo a woman. You got the finest vanilla and gourmet chocolate available. What's the plan?"

"For the auction, I need to bake these." I point to the cookbook with the Madeleines recipe.

She surveys it. "I thought you wanted to make cookies?"

"I do. These are cookies."

"They're cake."

"Cookies," I repeat.

She shakes her head. "My name is Madeleine, I'd know."

"You have a dog named Pop Tart. I hardly think that makes you an authority on naming conventions," I say with a playful smile.

"What's wrong with Pop Tart? She bounces like a pastry cake coming out of the toaster." Maddie demonstrates.

I laugh. "I even got a couple of the custom pans."

Arms across her chest, she says, "What if I don't want to? You're not the boss of me."

Then we both laugh because actually, I am or was.

"Why don't you want to make them?" I ask.

"It's just that my Gran used to on my birthday." Her chin trembles. "It's not the same this year. On the Christmas meter, Gran was a ten. I'm like a seven, verging toward an eight. Your mom tops Gran, which says a lot. On second thought, she'd be glad I'm here and want me to make the Madeleines."

The doorbell rings, interrupting what might very well be our first argument turned heart to heart.

"Do you like pizza?"

"That was customary every Friday along with a board game at the Tinsel residence, so yes."

When I open the door, the scent of dough and cheese fills the house.

When we dig in, Maddie says, "That settles it, you do know your way to a woman's heart."

Maddie's heart? I sure hope so.

CHAPTER 9

MADDIE

After Duffy and I have dinner, we bake dozens and dozens of Madeleine cookies with variations. Some we dip in chocolate. Others we sprinkle with powdered sugar, drizzle in white chocolate, or coat with almonds, and what he calls the *pièce de résistance*, a combination of all the above.

We're both overheated and possibly over-sugared. I'd love to plop onto the couch but should head back to Sleigh Bell Lodge. At the same time, I don't want tonight to end.

Instead of leaving the kitchen, we end up talking for a full hour and wander into the garage, where Duffy shows me his old toboggan. He digs up some snow gear for me and we head outside. I'm not sure where we find the energy, but we race up and down the hill at the end of Balsam Lane, laughing and whooping into the night.

It's so fun that I don't have time to be afraid of bears, moose, or whatever wildlife lurks in the wilds of North Pole, Alaska.

After numerous runs, I flop into the snow. He drops down next to me and we gaze at the stars.

"If we're lucky, we may see the northern lights," he says.

"It's beautiful here."

In my periphery, Duffy tilts his head to the side, facing me. "It sure is."

His gaze slides to mine and locks me in place, not that I can move after schlepping up the hill countless times.

He rolls in the snow to face me and we sit up. Eyes never wavering. A promise filling our mutual smiles. He angles my head toward his. Our mouths connect. His nose is cold but his lips warm me through.

His hands skim my shoulders and my mittens slide along his arms. It would be nice if we were in front of the fire, but Duffy's lips on mine set me ablaze. My pulse jingles and my thoughts recede. All that I know is that I want to spend more time with this man, baking, laughing, and kissing.

He draws back a few inches and his eyes sparkle. "Is this okay?"

"My Christmas cheer has reached newfound heights."

He chuckles and his mouth returns to mine.

I'm not sure where our fake relationship ends and this kiss begins, but it feels very real under the starry night sky.

❄

I wake up on Christmas Eve feeling like I'm floating in the clouds—very much like a snowflake, but not delicate or like I'm going to melt. Rather like I'm special, treasured. Throughout my dating history, I've never experienced this rush of excitement matched with comfort, connection, and contentment.

I'm not sure what to make of the kiss where no mistletoe was present. Duffy and my status is hazy even though the sky last night was perfectly clear. I've never seen so many stars or been kissed so ardently and with such blazing desire, even though we were in the snow. I'm surprised it didn't melt around us.

After taking Pop Tart for a walk around the block—and to

get a Christmas Eve cinnamon roll per tradition even though my sisters and I aren't together or with Gran—I dial them for a group video chat we scheduled. But the connection is bad, which might have something to do with another storm rolling in. I attempt to text, but it fails to send. Frowning, I continue to try until I have to meet Nicole to finalize the cookie count for the auction.

It's shortly after noontime when I return to the Sleigh Bell Lodge. Pop Tart is halfway through watching a Hallmark movie about a city girl celebrating a country Christmas. I snuggle up with her, feeling slightly homesick. This trip has been surprisingly wonderful and got me out of my pre-Christmas slump, but it's not the same without Anisette, Praline, and Tassie—Gran's sweeties.

The call still won't go through, so I get ready for the gala, channeling the fun my sisters and I used to have playing dress up and then in high school when we had dances and proms.

After applying light makeup and a red lip, I style my hair into loose curls. Finally, I put on my dress with a fitted cream-colored satin top and a long burgundy skirt that's cinched at my natural waist.

Taking a turn in front of the mirror, I ask Pop Tart, "What do you think?"

She gives one sharp bark of approval.

"I can always count on you."

The hotel room phone rings. The concierge tells me a gentleman is waiting for me downstairs. It must be Duffy picking me up for the Gala. Making sure Pop Tart has everything she needs, I promise we'll spend all of Christmas Day together and hurry downstairs.

When I reach the lobby, Duffy waits by the revolving door. Wearing a tuxedo with a burgundy pocket square that matches my skirt, he looks dashing.

As I approach, his eyes land on me and twinkle. His jaw

lowers and then his lips lift into a smile so big that I spot a dimple on his left cheek.

A pace away, Duffy reaches for my hands. His gaze drifts from my head to my toes and back again. "You look radiant."

My cheeks warm, making me second guess the dusting of blush. "You can thank Mary."

"No, Madeleine. That dress is all you." He wraps his arm around my waist and kisses my cheek. "You are beautiful."

My sisters have said as much, but I can't recall a man ever telling me that, no less one with Duffy's good looks. Never mind sugar plums, I'll have wedding bells dancing in my head when I go to sleep tonight.

An old-fashioned phone rings at the concierge desk and I startle, snapping me back to reality. We're faking dating, duh.

After we get into an awaiting car, I whisper, "Since we'll be in the public eye all night, if we're going to pull this off, we should know some things about each other."

His expression flickers. "Aside from the fact that you're a gorgeous, cookie-baking genius?"

Flustered, I breeze by his comment. "Have you ever had any odd jobs?"

"If you consider running a novelty coal company odd, then yes. The only other jobs I've had besides the family business and finance include being a paperboy and a backcountry hiking guide assistant in high school. I lasted exactly one day as a waiter in college. After that, I learned to invest. How about you?"

"Where do I start?"

We're nearly at the Arctic Arena and Convention Center, and I'm only on the first page of the assorted jobs I've held. My thoughts scramble and jumble. "We're almost there. Um, what's the worst present you ever got?"

"A deflated football wrapped in newspaper and duct tape from my buddy Mitch Calhoun. You?"

"There's no time. Do you consider yourself spontaneous or do you prefer to plan? Never mind, I know the answer to that."

Duffy takes my hands in his. "Until now, you've been the relaxed one and I've been quietly exploding."

"This is what you look like when you explode?"

"It's more of an implode—an inside job."

My voice rises with panic. "What if your mom finds out and—?"

Duffy draws me close and kisses my temple. "Maddie, you don't have anything to worry about."

The certainty in his words makes me believe him. But I'm nervous because I should've baked with my lucky apron.

As we cross the red, white, and green carpet into the venue, he says, "The theme this year is stars and stockings."

The walls are lined with Christmas stockings and everything sparkles.

Dressed up and out of context, it takes me a little while to recognize people from around town and from Stone's Coal company party.

We make small talk during the cocktail hour and then Mayor Donder announces it's time to gather for dinner. We find our assigned seats. I'm between Mrs. Stone and Duffy. Unfortunately, Porsha and three others sit across from us.

She bats her eyelashes at Cavell as her date tries to hold her hand.

It doesn't take long for us to learn that Porsha wanted Cavell back because she's broke, facts she not so subtly relays to her date. *Rude.* When he doesn't take the bait, she leaves halfway through the dinner. Everyone at the table lets out a collective sigh of relief.

Excitement builds when the auction starts. When the auctioneer calls out the massive amount of cookies for Nicholls' Candy Cane company, the bids come fast and furious. Nicole casts me an appreciative smile from across the room. I give a little fist pump to the air when it reaches the highest yet.

In addition to baked goods, there are locally made items like candles, wreaths, and ornaments—hence the bazaar part of the auction.

When Stone's Coal is called, the auctioneer's voice slows down. "The note here says to invite Cavell Stone to the stage."

He sets his napkin on the table and rises to his feet. Carol bounces in her seat.

From behind the mic, Duffy says, "This will only take a moment of your time. I attempted to bake coal-like cookies. As you can imagine, coal and cookies don't go together very well. Instead, I had someone help me make Madeleines. Now, before you argue about whether they're cookies or cake, it doesn't matter because Maddie and I go together very well. Even though we got off to a shaky and uncertain start, I dedicate this auction item to her with gratitude for showing me what forgiveness, trust, and truth really mean. Madeleine Tinsel is a special woman, and I'm grateful she's in my life. I wish for everyone in this room to be blessed with such an extraordinary Christmas gift."

Touched by this formerly gruff and grumpy man's sincere sentiment, tears well in my eyes, and joy brims inside.

The room erupts into cheers.

Carol squeezes my hand and whispers, "That makes two of us."

I glean that he told her the truth about us being a fake couple at first, but what we have is real.

After an evening filled with dancing and singing Christmas songs, hand in hand, Duffy and I stroll through town. We near the nativity scene outside the local church as the bells chime.

"It's Christmas Day," he says.

"Merry Christmas."

"Do you want to go to the midnight candlelit service?"

I nod. "I don't want tonight to end."

After we celebrate the birth of Jesus, Duffy and I return to his house. Pop Tart snuggles atop a tuffet by the dwindling fire. The lights on the tree twinkle. My heart is so full it nearly overflows.

We're both quiet on the way back to Sleigh Bell Lodge. When we reach the entrance, I don't let go of his hand.

I say, "Tonight was fun, and what you said meant a lot to me."

"It was all true."

"My flight back to New Hampshire is tomorrow evening."

"My VA is out of office until after the new year. Maybe she wants to stay here a few extra days." He suppresses a grin.

"She might like that."

"Maddie, I've struggled with trust issues. You changed that entirely. Every word of what I said earlier was true. I'd like you in my life, but not virtually."

I tip my gaze up to meet his. "I was a friendship and relationship ruiner, yet things with you are different. I shifted from feeling wounded to whole and excited about Christmas again."

"I don't think what we have is fake anymore."

Was it ever?

"Even if we leave Santa cookies, I worry we'll still end up with coal in our stockings."

Duffy chuckles. "Not if I have anything to say about that. After all, I'm the official supplier of coal to the North Pole."

This time, I laugh.

"What if we tell the truth?"

"I'd like that."

"I like you, Madeleine."

"I like you."

He says, "I'm not used to feelings this big."

"I know a lot about those, but I've never felt quite this way either."

"Like I found the one," we say at the same time.

We both laugh.

"Feelings like love," I add.

"Like love," Duffy repeats in a whisper.

Our lips meet in a goodnight kiss.

Glancing up as snowflakes dance from the sky, I spot a sprig of mistletoe.

Duffy beams a smile.

"See you tomorrow."

The church bells chime again.

I start to walk away, and over my shoulder, I say, "Er, I'll see you later."

Duffy clasps my hand, reeling me back. "Somehow, that mistletoe keeps following us around. I blame my mother."

"I thank her."

And our lips melt together in another kiss as we finish how we started, only I believe this is just the beginning.

EPILOGUE 1

MADDIE

The four squares on my phone fill with my family's faces: Anisette, Praline, Tassie, and Gran.

"Merry Christmas," we all say in turn.

I explain my bad connection when we'd tried to chat on Christmas Eve.

"You seem a lot merrier than the last time we talked," Ani says.

I shrug. "You can thank coal and cookies."

"You find some Christmas cheer up in Alaska?" Leeney asks.

Tassie gasps. "Did you fall in love?"

I open and close my mouth, unable to deny the truth.

My sisters gush and coo as I tell them about falling for Duffy, my boss—former boss. Nicole won the highest bid and accidentally-on-purpose let it slip that the Covert Cookie helped her achieve her goal, putting us both on the map—up here in the North Pole. I've had so many baking inquiries I can't keep up.

Last night, Duffy and I messaged through the virtual assistant portal about the future. I didn't renew my *00M* contract, but we made other plans. Stone's Coal Company has an empty building he said would make a great kitchen if I want to stick around.

I do. Very much.

Before getting off the phone with my family, Gran smiles and says, "Merry Christmas, My Sweeties."

As ever, we tell her we love her. But that's not all. What grows between Duffy and me is very real and very much shaped like love, and is as comforting as cookies on Christmas. Turns out I didn't need my lucky apron after all.

After the call, the virtual assistant portal dings with a notification.

> Cavell: I'm spending tomorrow with my girlfriend, so I no longer need that appointment with AccuPlex.

> 00M: Is that so? I'm glad to hear you found someone special. You must've been on Santa's good list.

> Cavell: She sure is special and beautiful, smart, funny, and makes the best cookies. Shh. Don't tell my mother.

> 00M: My lips are sealed. Er, except when we kiss.

> Cavell: Speaking of my mother, she told me the auction raised the most money for the charity in history.

> 00M: Interesting because Stone's Coal Company also posted a very large tax deduction.

> Cavell: What can I say, it was for a good cause.

> 00M: I'm glad I took the offer to bake for Nicholls' Candy Canes.

> Cavell: I'm glad I met you under the mistletoe.

> 00M: So are we still fake dating?

> Cavell: We're good at it,

> 00M: I do operate the Covert Cookie. I learned how to keep secrets and not lie.

> Cavell: Is there a difference?

> 00M: Absolutely, but I also may have exceeded expectations because you blew mine out of the water.

> Cavell: On that note, why are we messaging? We're on vacation. Bundle up, grab Pop Tart, and I'll have a hot cocoa waiting for you. Xo

And that does it. I'm officially in love.

When I get to Duffy's house, Pop Tart rushes up the walk, announcing our arrival.

The door opens and my very handsome former boss fills the entryway—we're partners now, having made plans to start our cookies and coal enterprise. Don't worry, not at the same time. But with his business skills and my baking ability, we might have a North Pole empire on our hands—or at least a great excuse to spend more time together working on a real relationship.

"Merry Christmas," I say.

His lips quirk and he replies with the same, but doesn't move from the spot.

Peering over his shoulder where Pop Tart waits patiently, I ask, "Do I need to use a special password or code to get inside?"

"Nope."

"Sing a Christmas carol? Do a jolly dance?"

"We did a lot of that last night." He draws me close.

"Then are you going to let me in?"

He points to the upper part of the door's frame.

"Did a Christmas elf put that there?"

"Could've been Mrs. Claus."

I narrow my eyes. "I do enjoy our mistletoe kisses, so I suppose I wouldn't mind . . ."

When our lips meet, a happy little giggle comes from inside the house that sounds suspiciously like Carol, the matchmaker, followed by a yap from her newest little elf accomplice—Pop Tart.

As the kiss builds, everything fades away except the present and the future, which I am certain includes this man whose love feels even better than a gift wrapped in a bow.

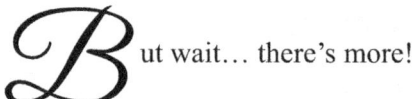ut wait… there's more!

EPILOGUE 2: ONE YEAR LATER

*K*eep reading for a special recipe featured in *Madeleine's Mistletoe Meet Cute…*

RECIPE

Madeleine cookies are light and airy yet buttery and go great with tea, cocoa, or as a special addition to your holiday baking cookie plate. You can dust them with powdered sugar, drizzle them in chocolate, or get creative and dip them in white chocolate and add festive sprinkles.

- Prep Time: 15 minutes
- Refrigeration Time: 1 hour
- Cook Time: 10-12 minutes
- Total Time: Approximately 1 ½ hours
- Yields: 18-20 cookies

Special items needed:

- Madeleine pan
- Flour sifter
- Wire rack to cool

Ingredients:

- 8 tablespoons of unsalted butter + 2 tablespoons for the pan
- 2 eggs, room temperature
- 1/2 cup sugar
- 2 teaspoons lemon zest
- 2 teaspoons vanilla extract
- 1 cup all-purpose flour, sifted + extra for lightly dusting the pan
- 1/2 teaspoon baking powder
- 1/4 teaspoon salt
- See the description above for topping options

Instructions:

1. Melt the butter, and set it aside to cool slightly (but don't allow it to resolidify).
2. Whisk the sugar, eggs, lemon zest, and vanilla in a large mixing bowl.
3. In a separate bowl, combine the flour, baking powder, and salt. Sift the mixture and then, working with 1/3 at a time, gently fold it into the wet mixture until combined. Add in cooled liquid butter.
4. Chill the batter for 30 minutes.
5. Preheat the oven to 350 degrees F, grease a madeleine pan, and dust it with flour, tapping out excess for a fine layer.
6. Scoop 1 1/2 tablespoons of batter into each well of the pan or three-quarters of the way full. Don't fill to the top.
7. Bake until puffed and golden brown around the edges and springy to the touch, approximately 10 to 12 minutes. Transfer to a wire rack to cool, and dust with powdered sugar or other fun toppings as described above!

MADELEINE'S MISTLETOE MEET CUTE

Madeleines are best enjoyed fresh, but they will keep in an airtight container at room temperature for three days.

If you make this recipe, please share on social media and tag me @elliehallauthor everywhere!

If you enjoyed *Madeleine's Mistletoe Meet Cute*, jingle all the way through the festive season with ELEVEN more Christmas novelettes that are like little bites of sweet and swoony delight.

These heartwarming and feel-good romances feature second chances, enemies turned lovers, fake dating adventures, and more, all wrapped up in the cozy merriment of the holidays. Plus, there's a cookie recipe in each book! Find out more on the Christmas Kisses & Cookie Crumbs sales page.

Ellie's Christmas Romance Books

Madeleine's Mistletoe Meet Cute is part of a new meet cute mishaps series, coming soon. In the meantime, if you want more Christmas romance, I have ten books filled with festive, feel-good fun + an entire Christmas series called the Costa Brothers, plus a companion cookbook. Take a look at elliehallauthor.com/christmasromance

ABOUT THE AUTHOR

Ellie Hall is a USA Today bestselling author. If only that meant she could wear a tiara and get away with it ;) She loves puppies, books, and the ocean. Writing sweet romance with lots of firsts and fizzy feels brings her joy. Oh, and chocolate chip cookies are her fave.

Ellie believes in dreaming big, working hard, and lazy Sunday afternoons spent with her family and dog in gratitude for God's grace.

Let's Connect

Do you love sweet, swoony romance?
Stories with happy endings?
Falling in love?

Please subscribe to my newsletter to receive updates about my latest books, exclusive extras, deals, and other fun and sparkly things, including a FREE eBook, the *The Secret Book Boyfriend*! Get your free copy here: www.elliehall.com 🩶

ALSO BY ELLIE HALL

All books are clean and wholesome, Christian faith-friendly and without mature content but filled with swoony kisses and happily ever afters. Books are listed under series in recommended reading order.

-select titles available in audiobook, paperback, hardcover, and large print-

The Only Us Sweet Billionaire Series

Only a Date with a Billionaire

Only a Kiss with a Billionaire

Only a Night with a Billionaire

Only Forever with a Billionaire

Only Love with a Billionaire

Only Christmas with a Billionaire

Only New Year with a Billionaire

The Only Us Sweet Billionaire series box set (books 2-5) + a bonus scene!

Hawkins Family Small Town Romance Series

Second Chance in Hawk Ridge Hollow

Finding Forever in Hawk Ridge Hollow

Coming Home to Hawk Ridge Hollow

Falling in Love in Hawk Ridge Hollow

Christmas in Hawk Ridge Hollow

The Hawk Ridge Hollow Series Complete Collection Box Set (books 1-5)

♥

The Blue Bay Beach Reads Romance Series

Summer with a Marine

Summer with a Rock Star

Summer with a Billionaire

Summer with the Cowboy

Summer with the Carpenter

Summer with the Doctor

Books 1-3 Box Set

Books 4-6 Box Set

Ritchie Ranch Clean Cowboy Romance Series

Rustling the Cowboy's Heart (Book 1)

Lassoing the Cowboy's Heart (Book 2)

Trusting the Cowboy's Heart (Book 3)

Kissing the Christmas Cowboy

Loving the Cowboy's Heart

Wrangling the Cowboy's Heart

Charming the Cowboy's Heart

Saving the Cowboy's Heart

Ritchie Ranch Romance Books 1-4 Box Set

Falling into Happily Ever After Rom Com

An Unwanted Love Story

An Unexpected Love Story

An Unlikely Love Story

An Accidental Love Story

An Impossible Love Story

An Unconventional Christmas Love Story

Forever Marriage Match Romantic Comedy Series

Dare to Love My Grumpy Boss

Dare to Love the Guy Next Door

Dare to Love My Fake Husband

Dare to Love the Guy I Hate

Dare to Love My Best Friend

Home Sweet Home Series

Mr. and Mrs. Fix It Find Love

Designing Happily Ever After

The DIY Kissing Project

The True Romance Renovation: Christmas Edition

Extreme Heart Makeover

Building What's Meant to Be

The Costa Brothers Cozy Christmas Comfort Romance Series

Tommy & Merry and the 12 Days of Christmas

Bruno & Gloria and the 5 Golden Rings

Luca & Ivy and the 4 Calling Birds

Gio & Joy and the 3 French Hens

Paulo & Noella and the 2 Turtle Doves

Nico & Hope and the Partridge in the Pear Tree

The Love List Series

The Swoon List

The Not Love List

The Crush List

The Kiss List

The Naughty or Nice List

Love, Laughs & Mystery in Coco Key

*Clean romantic comedy, family secrets, and treasure *These books should be read in the following order:*

The Romance Situation

The Romance Fiasco

The Romance Game

The Romance Gambit

The Christmas Romance Wish

The Nebraska Knights Holiday Hockey Romance Series

Stupid Cupid

Redd, Whit & Blue

The Kiss Class

Margo & the Faux Good Luck Beau

The Ex-Puck Bunny

Love at First Skate (Tie-In)

Love in Hockey Town (Ties in to the Nebraska Knights)

His Jersey

My Wife

Her Goal

On the Hunt for Love

Sweet, Small Town & Southern

The Grump & the Girl Next Door

The Bitter Heir & the Beauty

The Secret Son & the Sweetheart

The Ex-Best Friend & the Fake Fiancee

The Best Friend's Brother & the Brain

Don't You Forget About Tea (Tie-In)

SoCal Summer Kisses

We Go Together

The One I Want

Hopelessly Devoted

Stand Alone Titles

Happily Ever Haunted (a romcom - ghost mashup)

The Secret Book Boyfriend (small town, grumpy sunshine)

Madeleine's Mistletoe Meet Cute (small town, mistaken identity)

Visit www.elliehallauthor.com or your favorite retailer for more.

If you love my books, please leave a review on your favorite retailer's website! Thank you! 🖤 Ellie

P.S. I have a clean fantasy and paranormal romance pen name: E. Hall that you might enjoy (best read in listed order):

The Court of Crown and Compass Series

Fae of Light and Shadow (prequel)

Fae of the North (book 1)

Fae of the West (book 2)

Fae of the South (book 3)

Fae of the East (book 4)

RIP Magic Academy Reform School Series
Law & Disorder (book 1)

Crime & Curses (book 2)

Mayhem & Magic (book 3)

Shifter Diaries
Life Fated (book 1)

Lies Tamed (book 2)

Loss Hunted (book 3)

Love United (book 4)

Made in the USA
Coppell, TX
14 December 2024